Bruno
Has One Hundred
FRIENDS

Francesca Pirrone

Clavis

NEW YORK

Bruno is on his way to go fishing with his friends when on the road he finds a strange object.

What's that?

Curious, he picks it up. As soon as he's got it in his hand, it flashes bright.

How beautiful! Bruno thinks.

Renzo calls out to him. "Where are you? We are waiting for you!"

"Go ahead. I'll catch up to you," Bruno answers.

He lies down and starts inspecting the strange box.

Inside, Bruno finds extraordinary things: pictures he's never seen, words he's never read, sounds he's never heard.

But above all, **so many friends!**

Renzo and Rico come back to see what Bruno is up to.
"What have you got there?" they ask.

"**Look!**" Bruno replies, and full of pride he shows them
the magical box. "I think it's called a phone."

"What's it for?" the other bears ask.

"It's for making lots of friends," Bruno answers.

"But we're your friends!" Renzo and Rico exclaim.

"Yes, but there's only two of you.
Now I've got at least **one hundred friends** all over the world."

From that moment on, Bruno is always busy
with his phone.

From early in the morning till late in the evening, he's chatting,
watching movies, or listening to music. And his list of friends is growing!

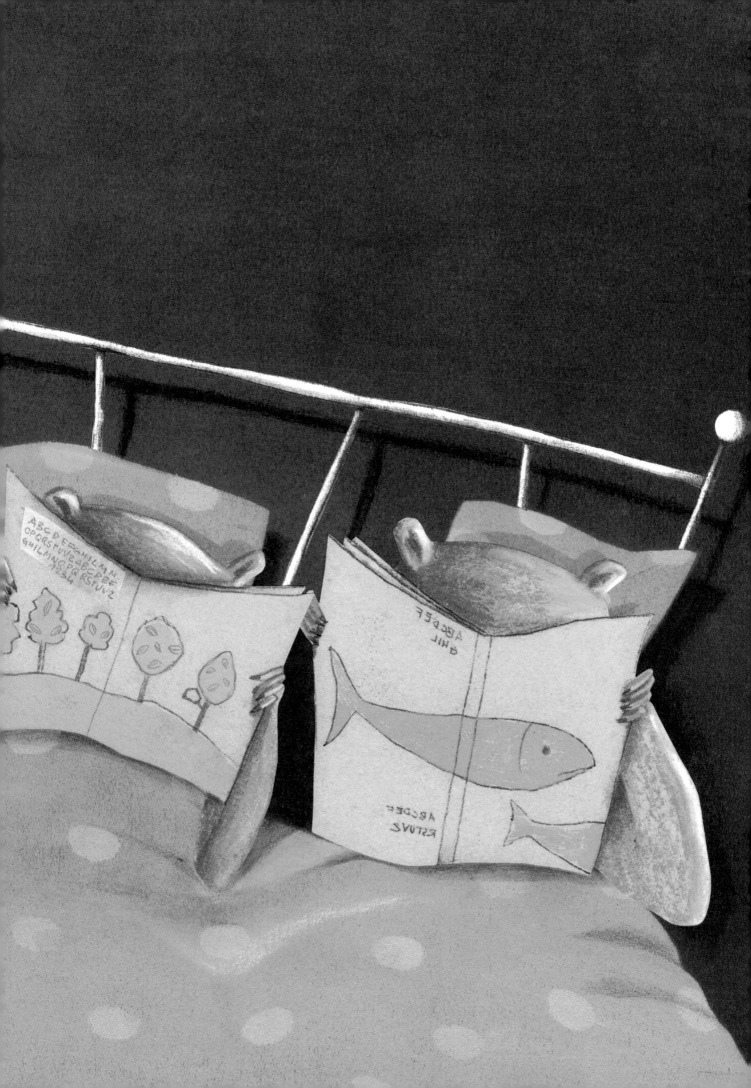

Renzo and Rico are worried.
They want to have their old friend back.
So they invite him to go and collect honey together
and to have a picnic in the forest.
They've packed all of Bruno's favorite snacks.
But it's all in vain. Bruno has no interest in anything but his phone.

He is too busy for anyone else.

But then something happens.
The magical box doesn't light up anymore.

"What happened?"

Bruno asks himself aloud.
"Where are all my friends?"
He gives the phone a shake.

Bruno is worried. He runs outside and holds the phone high above his head, turning it this way and that.

He runs until he comes upon Renzo and Rico.
"What are you doing?" they ask.
"I'm trying to get reception before I lose all my friends!

I had close to five hundred and now they're all gone!"

Tears are flowing down Bruno's cheeks.

Renzo and Rico gather up Bruno in a big hug.
"I was wrong," Bruno says, staring at his feet in shame.

"You are my real friends!"

"That's right!" Renzo and Rico are laughing.
"We will always be right here for you!"

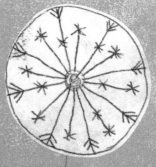
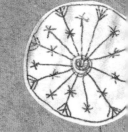
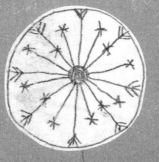
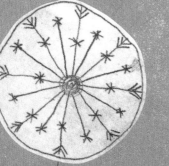

"And now let's go and have some fun," Rico says.

"Yes!" Bruno exclaims.

"Who needs one hundred virtual friends when I have the two of you!"

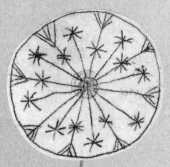
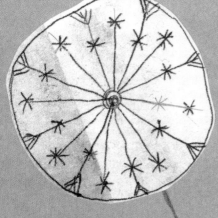

Originally published as *Bruno heeft wel 100 vrienden* in Belgium and Holland
by Clavis Uitgeverij, Hasselt—Amsterdam, 2017
English translation from the Dutch by Clavis Publishing Inc., New York

Visit us on the Web at www.clavis-publishing.com.

Bruno Has One Hundred Friends written and illustrated by Francesca Pirrone

ISBN 978-1-60537-405-5 (hardcover edition)
ISBN 978-1-60537-504-5 (softcover edition)

This book was printed in July 2019 at Nikara, M. R. Štefánika 858/25, 963 01 Krupina, Slovakia.

First Edition
10 9 8 7 6 5 4 3 2 1